E
BRO

THROUGH THE MAGIC MIRROR

Anthony Browne

GREENWILLOW BOOKS, New York

 First published in Great Britain in 1976 by Hamish Hamilton Children's Books. First published in the United States in 1977 by Greenwillow Books; reissued 1992.

1350 Avenue of the Americas, New York, NY 10019. Printed in Scotland by Cambus Litho
First Edition 1 2 3 4 5 6 7 8 9 10

Library of Congress Cataloging-in-Publication Data: Browne, Anthony. Through the magic mirror / by Anthony Browne.
p. cm. Summary: A young boy steps through his mirror into a world which looks the same but is slightly different.
ISBN 0-688-10725-7. [1. Fantasy.] I. Title. PZ7.B81984Th 1992 [E]—dc20 90-23166 CIP AC

Toby sat in the big chair. He was fed up. Fed up with books, fed up with toys, fed up with everything.

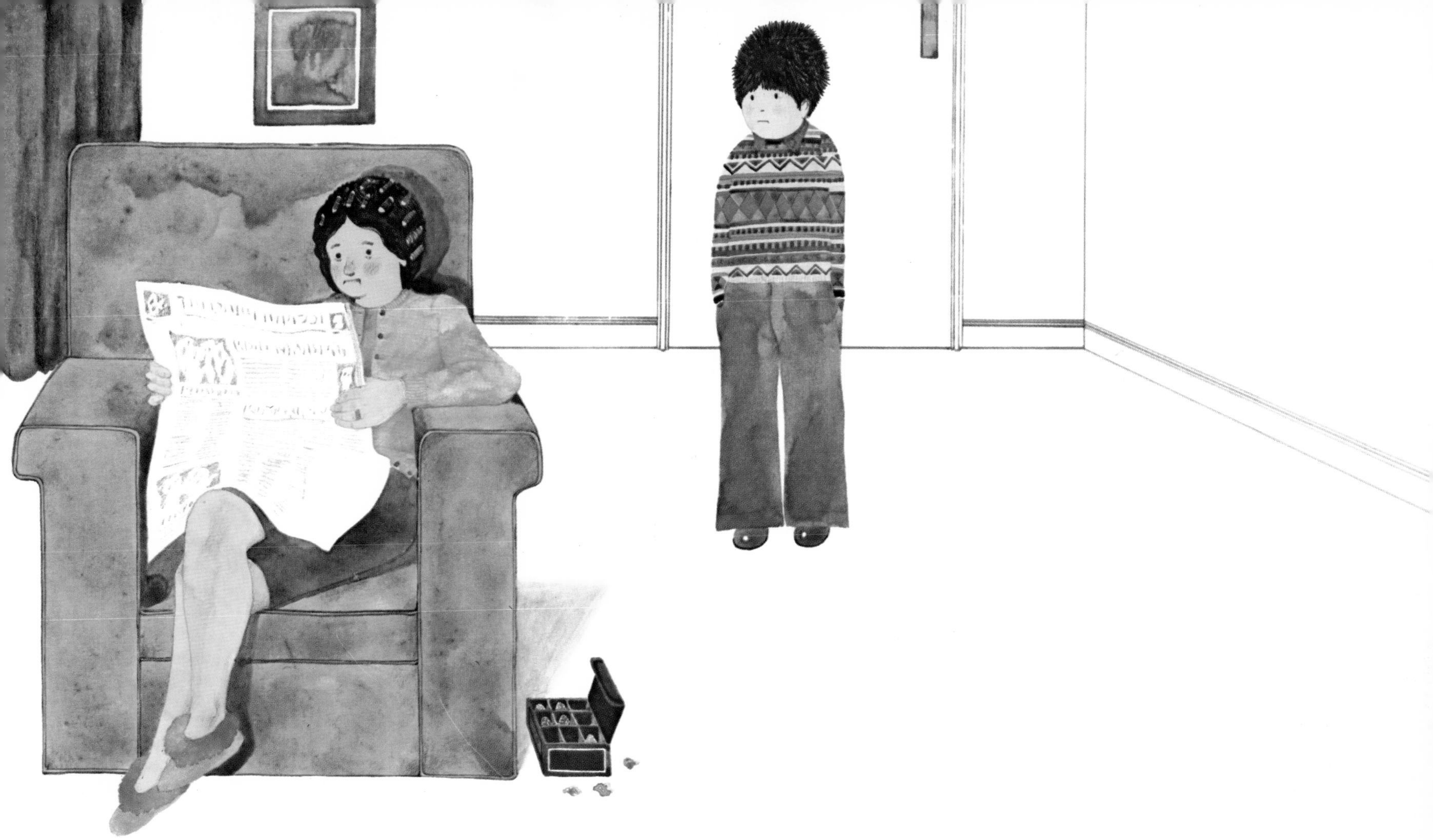

He went into the living room. Nothing was happening there.

Going back upstairs, he saw himself in a mirror.

Something looked very strange
What was wrong?

He put out his hand to touch the mirror – and walked right through it!

He was out in the street. It seemed like the same old street, but was it?

An invisible man passed by.

On the corner was an easel. On the easel was
a painting of a painting of a painting.

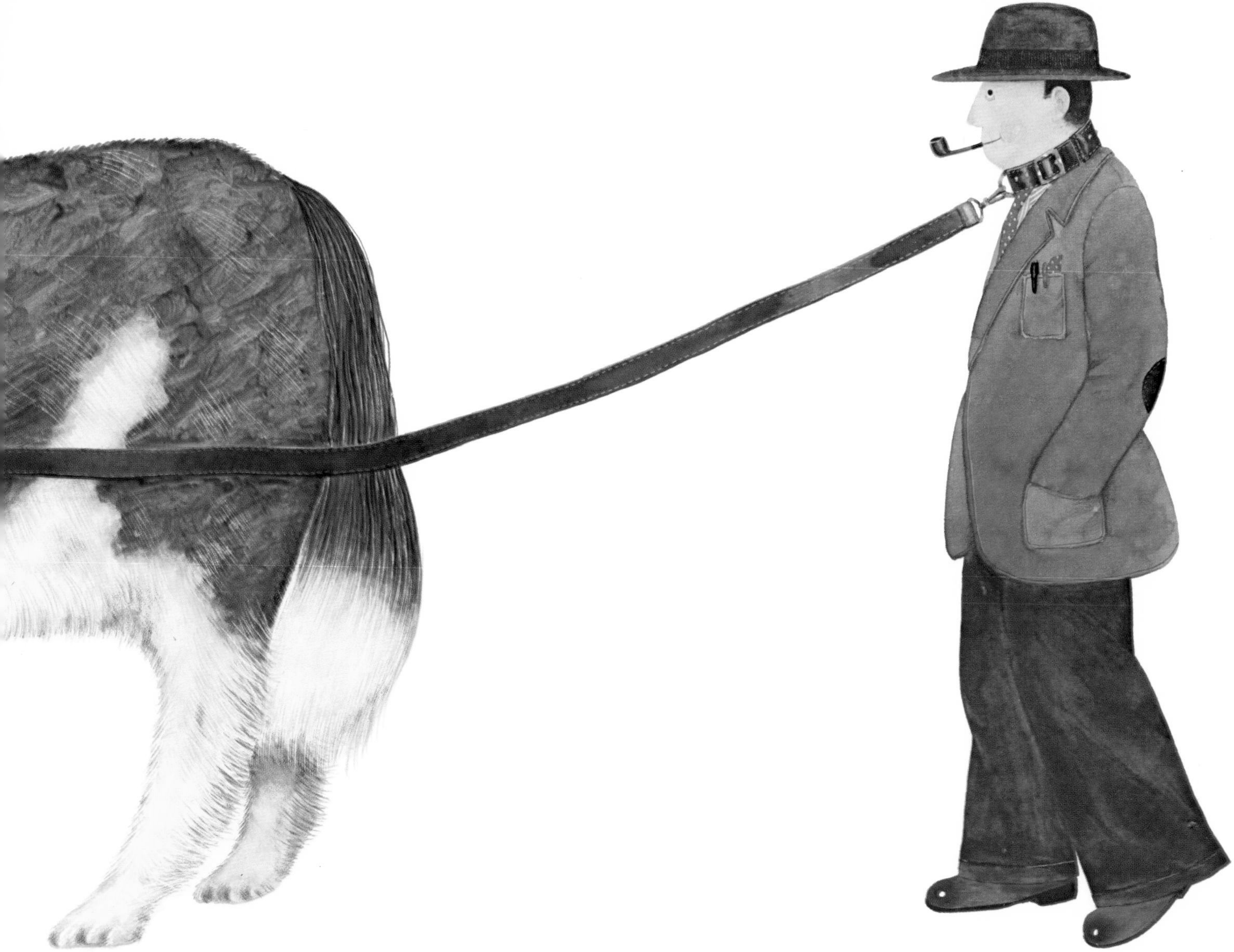

Just then a dog came along, taking a man for a walk.

Toby walked on. Two men were painting a fence.

Toby took another look. He could hardly believe what he saw.

Suddenly the sky became dark as a flock of choirboys flew overhead

A terrified cat darted past, chased by a gang of hungry mice.

At the bus stop Toby saw a queue of funny people.

They seemed a bit mixed up.

And the traffic seemed somehow different.

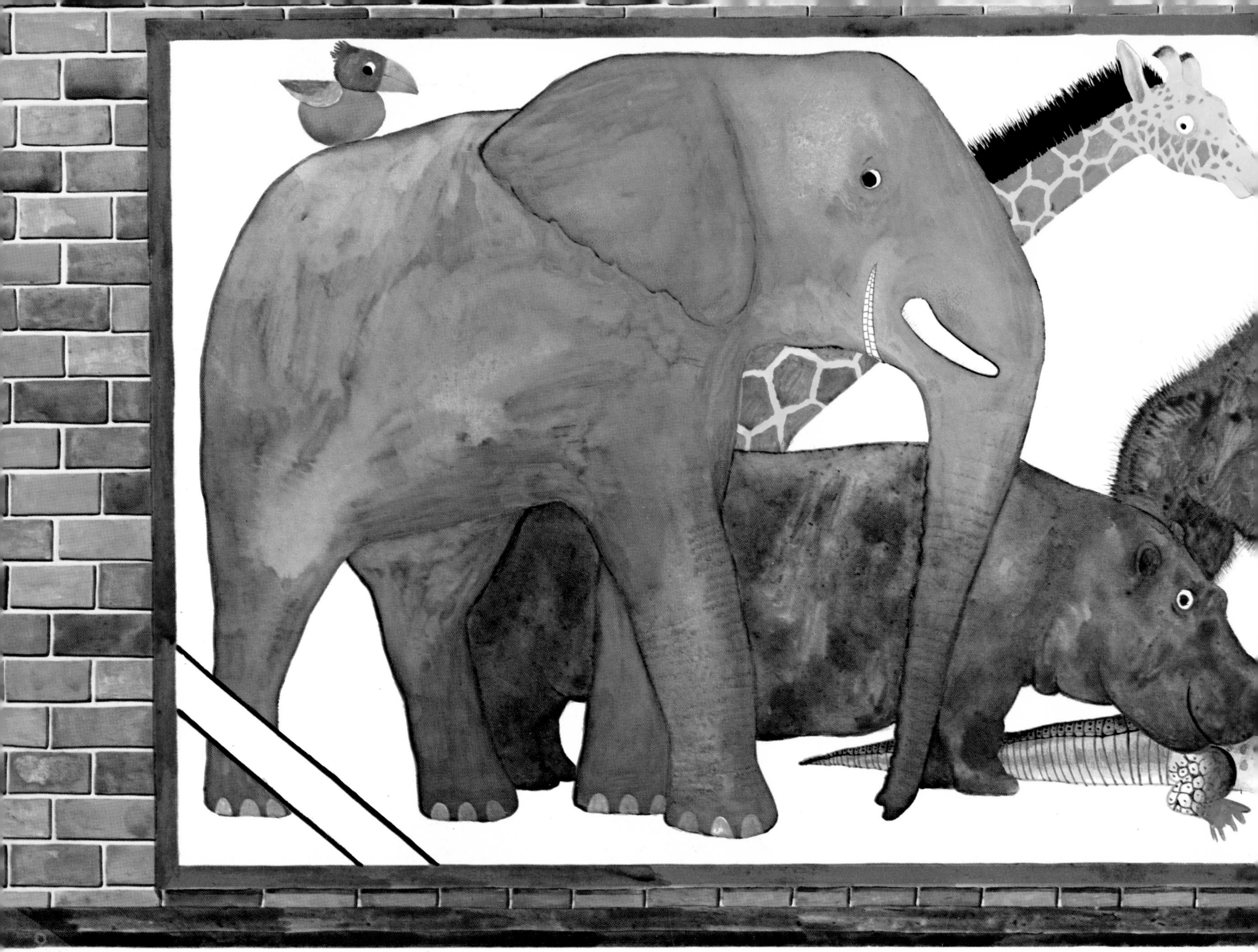

Across the road Toby saw a poster for the zoo.

But what was happening?

Toby ran as fast as he could.

Where was that mirror?

Of course, there it was,
right behind him.

Toby stepped through, back
into his own house.

He turned around and looked at himself in the mirror.
When he saw his face, he smiled.

Then he ran down to tea.